What in the whole weird world is *that*?

Something was sticking out from the tile on the bathroom wall. It was a long pink tongue.

A bloodred stone was lodged in it like a great big cough drop.

"Gol-*leeee!*" Marthur yelled. It was so bedazzling she had to shield her eyes.

Her imagination went nuts. *What's attached to this thing? What if it's connected to a monster that's about to burst through the wall and start slurping up kids? Jeez!*

"You're a Snapdragon," she reminded herself. But she couldn't save the whole school from the monster in the wall.

Still, she had to warn everybody!

The Spoon
IN THE
Bathroom Wall

TONY JOHNSTON

The Spoon
IN THE
Bathroom Wall

HARCOURT, INC.

Orlando Austin New York San Diego Toronto London

www.HarcourtBooks.com

First Harcourt paperback edition 2006

Epigraph by Langston Hughes. "Dreams" from
The Collected Poems of Langston Hughes by Langston Hughes,
copyright © 1994 by The Estate of Langston Hughes. Used by
permission of Alfred A. Knopf, a division of Random House, Inc.,
and Harold Ober Associates Incorporated.

The Library of Congress has cataloged the hardcover edition as follows:
Johnston, Tony, 1942–
The spoon in the bathroom wall/by Tony Johnston.
p.   cm.
Summary: Living in the boiler room of the school where her father
is janitor seems normal to fourth grader Martha Snapdragon, until
she has experiences with an evil principal, the class bully, and a
mysterious giant spoon, all reminiscent of the Arthurian legends.
[1. Fathers and daughters—Fiction.   2. Bullying—Fiction.
3. School principals—Fiction.   4. Schools—Fiction.
5. Magic—Fiction.]   I. Title.
PZ7.J6478Spo   2005
[Fic]—dc22   2004017415
ISBN-13: 978-0-15-205292-8   ISBN-10: 0-15-205292-5
ISBN-13: 978-0-15-205625-4 pb   ISBN-10: 0-15-205625-4 pb

Text set in Legacy Serif Book
Designed by Linda Lockowitz

A   C   E   G   H   F   D   B

Printed in the United States of America

For Jeannette Larson, a king among editors

For Larry Onderdonk, who loves bacon

For Martha Tolles, who always looks to the positive

*And with thanks to the other wizards
of our writers' group*

T. H. White, in memoriam

DREAMS

Hold fast to dreams
For if dreams die
Life is a broken-winged bird
That cannot fly.

Hold fast to dreams
For when dreams go
Life is a barren field
Frozen with snow.

LANGSTON HUGHES

1

Martha Snapdragon (rhymes with *wagon*) lived with her father, Luther Snapdragon, in the boiler room of Horace E. Bloggins (rhymes with *noggins*) School. Nobody remembers what Horace E. Bloggins did to get a school named after him. Maybe it was for surviving the name Bloggins.

The boiler room was like an oversize cracker box. A maze of steam pipes ran side to side along the walls, up and down, every which way, carrying steam to all the other rooms, heating the school in winter. Unfortunately, Horace E. Bloggins School was as old as mold. Nothing worked right, especially not the ancient steam pipes. So they also heated the place in summer.

The constant *blup* and *phlut* of water gargled in the metal throats of the boiler-room pipes. Some clunked and clanked in an everlasting racket. Year-round, Martha and her father wore earmuffs to muffle the cacophony. (It didn't help much.) But their voices got muffled, too, so they had conversations like this:

Luther: "How was school, dear?"

Martha: "I don't think so."

Luther: "Drat! Whacked my finger with the hammer!"

Martha: "That's nice, Daddy."

On a daily basis, the Snapdragons were nearly cooked, like crustaceans in a pot. They sweated a lot and their skin was as pink as SPAM. But even though the boiler room was sweltering hot, they were grateful that the principal, Dr. Klunk (rhymes with *junk*), gave them a roof over their heads, as part of Luther's (very low) pay.

Luther Snapdragon was the school janitor, on call both day and night. Dr. Klunk woke him up whenever he felt like it (sometimes just for fun). Luther didn't mind. Times were tough and he was happy to have a job and a place to live for his little daughter and himself.

Martha's mother had died some years before. Since then Luther Snapdragon had seemed a bit lost. But he loved his daughter and tried valiantly in his cloudy way to take care of her.

"Look to the positive, Martha," he often said, trying to keep their spirits up. "Imagine something wonderful about our little home."

Martha was always hungry. So she would scrunch her eyes shut and imagine her favorite thing, bacon, looped over every inch of pipe. Scrumptious bacon, popping and sizzling.

But the Snapdragons were too poor to buy bacon. Sometimes they poached eggs in a pot on the pipework instead. They had to sling their laundry there, too, both clean and dirty. The light was bad, so often they wore dirty clothes instead of clean. Oh well. That didn't matter. They had each other.

Martha was proud of her father for his hard work and devotion (thirty-seven years come July) to Horace E. Bloggins School. She knew how hard he worked, for the school and for her. So she tried to take care of him, too.

Bloggins was a good school in lots of ways. It had some great teachers. It had nice lawns. And trees. It had cool brick hallways

with great sayings chiseled into them. Sayings like:

LEARNING IS GOOD.
SLACKING IS BAD.
MATH IS TONS OF FUN.
READ YOUR BRAINS LOOSE.

One bad thing about Horace E. Bloggins
School was Dr. Klunk. The principal was
pudgy and pasty and bald as a bottle, with
beastly little eyes like mean raisins. He
looked like the Pillsbury Doughboy stuffed
into a suit.

Dr. Klunk wasn't a doctor at all. He lied
about that. He wasn't a real principal. Big
fat fib. But he *was* a sneak. That's how he'd
squirmed himself into this Place of Power.

Dr. Klunk wanted to boss everybody.
And to be rich. But he was too sneaky to do
his own dirty work. He got the school bully,

Rufus Turk (rhymes with *jerk*), to spy on teachers and dig out their secrets. Then he could *really* boss them around (and pay them less). Rufus stole kids' lunch money for Klunk. In exchange he and his gang could do whatever they pleased.

Rufus was a runty kid, like Napoléon. He had a pinchy face like a boll weevil, ratty little teeth, and hair the color of an orangutan. It was unfair to compare him with orangutans, for those apes are gentle creatures. Rufus wasn't.

Once he'd stuck a kindergartner in a tree. He laughed like crazy while the little kid bawled. Dr. Klunk had ordered a pizza and plunked a chair nearby. He laughed, too, spitting out pepperoni. Martha couldn't bear it. She'd scrambled up, helped the kid down, and got one thousand demerits.

Kids didn't bother to tell their parents what went on at Bloggins. They used to, but their parents didn't believe them. They believed the principal—imagine! Martha didn't tell her father much, either. She didn't want to worry him. Besides, Luther Snapdragon was too kind to think that anybody could be so evil. "Look to the positive," Luther would have told her. "At least you *have* a principal."

Rufus loved to terrorize everybody. But mostly he loved to torment Martha Snapdragon. Just seeing her fried his brain with anger. Sometimes he tied Martha's shoelaces together. Then he gave her a shove. Poor Martha hopped a lot, then fell on her face and got all scraped up. One or two of the other kids laughed, but mostly they felt sorry for her. They liked Martha. She'd saved lots of them from Klunk and Rufus. (So Rufus hated her even more.)

Rufus also squished chewing gum into her hair. Though she cut it out as carefully as she could, Rufus kept sticking gum into it. Her hair always looked like a horse had chewed it.

"You're nuthin' but a *brain-o*!" Rufus hollered whenever he saw Martha. "And your father's the janitor! Har! Har! Har!" (His father made movies and went to parties and ate sushi with movie stars and did other important stuff.)

Martha felt glum. Why was Rufus after *her*? She had no idea. She hated the taunts and the shoving and the chewing-gum treatment, but she hated jeers about her father more. And she couldn't stand that ruffian bullying little kids. But Martha was just one girl—usually limp as uncooked bacon, from sleepless nights and skimpy meals. She just had to take it. Martha couldn't do anything about Rufus. She could do even less about Dr. Klunk.

ii

In spite of everything, Martha Snap-dragon liked school. She did her lessons cheerfully (though sleepily) and earned high marks. She was the best pupil in the fourth grade; Rufus was the worst. Most kids looked up to Martha, she was so smart. (And she never showed off about it.)

English was as easy for her as pouncing is for a cat. She was a whiz in math—for years she'd been figuring out the price per ounce at the market so she could buy the cheapest items. Science, however, was Martha's best subject. And her favorite.

Her science teacher, Mrs. Ferlin (rhymes

with *Merlin*), taught with such pizzazzle, the kids thought she used magic. When they studied space, Mrs. Ferlin levitated potatoes of different sizes into their proper places around a floating pumpkin, to represent the planets zooming around the sun. All the kids *ooh*ed and *aah*ed. When the lesson was done, they ate mashed potatoes and pumpkin pie (with whipped cream).

Dr. Klunk was sure Mrs. Ferlin was up to something BAD. But hard as he tried, he could never catch her at it. For spite he called her just plain Ferlin. Pretty soon everybody did. She didn't care. She was peculiar—in a good way. Martha wanted to be just like her.

Though Martha was happy in her studies at Horace E. Bloggins, she dreaded seeing Rufus. One day she was playing four square with her friends. She spotted Rufus and his hoodlums swaggering around. Their T-shirts were loose. Their pants were so baggy, they were falling off. Their smirks said, Don't we look cool? (They didn't.)

They swarmed up to Martha.

"Hey, brain-o!" Rufus roared. He was wearing a stolen Dodgers cap.

Martha's heart banged like a bongo drum. Her hands went clammy. What was he going to do? She braced for a ruthless heckling—or a general pulverizing.

"So," jeered Rufus, "how's old genius, intellect, learned, brilliant, nimble-wit, clever-as-they-come, sharp-as-a-tack, smart-as-a-whip little daughter-of-a-jani*tor, Mar-thur*?"

(Rufus didn't really know what all those words meant. He was spouting them from a thesaurus he'd stolen.)

"Fine," said Martha in the strongest voice she could muster. "And my name is

MARTHA," she added proudly. (It was also her dear deceased mother's name.)

"MAR-THUR! MAR-THUR! MAR-THUR!" Rufus bellowed.

"MAR-THUR! MAR-THUR! MAR-THUR!" chanted his toughs.

Dr. Klunk was walking by. He jumped right in. "MAR-THUR! MAR-THUR! MAR-THUR!" Then he waddled to the office and boomed the name over the loudspeaker.

Like a bad case of chicken pox, the awful new label raged through school. By lunchtime Martha was as forgotten as Horace E. Bloggins. Now she was Marthur, a name as heavy as mud. She'd rather have been pulverized by a busload of bullies, clobbered by a clan of Klunks.

After school Martha wandered off by herself down a dim and lonely corridor. She wanted to be alone. She didn't want to hear that horrid new name.

Suddenly—how funny—she felt a strong pull to look up. So she did. She noticed a curious saying chiseled into a slab of bricks above her. A saying she'd never seen before:

The King Is Coming—
and It's About Time.

(It was worked up in weird old-fashioned writing.) She wondered, *How did I ever miss this?*

Here at Horace E. Bloggins—a king? What a silly thing! Kings were for *old* places, like England or Persia or maybe even Tasmania. Martha didn't really believe it. Still, for a moment she was full of hope. She felt certain that kings were better trained than principals. Better than *her* principal, anyway.

A king would make things good for the kids at Bloggins. She thought, *Well, if he's coming, he'd better come NOW.* Maybe a king could even help her with Rufus and Klunk.

iii

Martha slogged along in a daze of gloom. She didn't feel like going home to the boiler room. Her father would read her face like three-inch headlines and know that something was wrong. Then she'd have to fudge about the Marthur incident. But sooner or later, he'd hear about it. The jibe about being the daughter-of-a-janitor would jolt him like a jab in the ribs.

"I'll go see Ferlin," she muttered. "If anybody can perk me up, she can." Martha walked up to Ferlin's door and nearly bonked into it, she was so lost in her worries.

"Hello, Martha," called Ferlin from inside. "Come on in."

That's so odd, Martha thought. *How does she know I'm here?* She opened the door and went in.

The science room had a strange feeling about it, as if magic had sparkled up from Somewhere and shimmered all through it. If there *was* magic around, however, it was not powerful enough to keep things clean. There were messes all over the place (even on the ceiling). There were artifacts and relics scattered about and wildlife on the loose. A sign on Ferlin's desk said: ENJOY THE WEIRDNESS.

Normally, Martha would have first talked with the griffin (a regal beast—half eagle, half lion), which was daintily nibbling figs off Ferlin's desk. The griffin was wonky for figs. Whenever it smelled one, even a mile away, the creature sallied forth to find it. (The griffin always stayed stock-still around Dr. Klunk. He thought it was a fake; the kids knew it wasn't.)

This day Martha didn't even glance at the griffin. "How did you know I was outside?" she asked Ferlin.

"Sensed it. I'm loaded with sense!" Ferlin laughed heartily.

Ferlin was wearing her favorite outfit: a plum-colored gown spangled with Oreos in orbit and a hat made from a neon-orange construction cone. Her earrings were over-size lumps resembling (or *were* they?) asteroids. Her white hair shot out in a frenzy, like electrified cotton candy. Her eyes flared as though she were constantly hatching plots. (She was.)

"You look a bit dolorous," said Ferlin.

"Huh?"

"Downcast. Despondent. In the dumps. It's the name, isn't it?"

"You heard it on the loudspeaker, right?"

"I didn't hear a thing. I had my earplugs in earlier—to enjoy the gorgeosity of SILENCE." (Her earplugs were big fat lima beans that glowed like little lightbulbs.)

"So how come you know about the name?"

"Who can say?" Ferlin said mysteriously, gazing off into space. Ferlin always knew stuff before you told her. "I think *Marthur* has a certain *je ne sais quoi*," she went on, fumbling for something in her voluminous purse. "Rhymes with *Arthur*. He was quite a king."

King! Martha thought. She was about to mention the odd saying on the wall, but Ferlin kept right on talking.

"Your new name could be worse."

"Not much." Martha moped.

"Could be—Martholomew." Ferlin's eyes glittered like glass.

"*No way!* I'd rather kiss a slug than be called *that*!"

"Then be grateful it's Marthur."

"I guess I'll have to be."

Ferlin kept rummaging in her handbag. "What I have in here is absolutely hush-hush." She lowered her voice. "My reputation's already a bit iffy."

"Hush-hush," Marthur repeated. She could hardly wait to see what it was.

"Ah-*ha*!" Ferlin cried suddenly. "*There* you are!"

She pulled out a violently purple egg carton, embellished with the letters *X-C* and a funny emblem that looked like a weird old spoon. She took the eggs out of the carton one by one and placed them precariously on a slanted desktop.

"Look out! They're going to smash!" yelped Marthur. She dashed to stop the eggs' roll. But before she could catch them, they sprouted legs, stood up, and tap danced.

"Eggs with legs!" Marthur clapped happily. "I love them!"

"I knew you would," said Ferlin. "Care to place them back in there? They were running around all morning."

Beaming like a jack-o'-lantern, Marthur carefully put the eggs into the purple carton. One kept trying to escape. "NO NAP!" it grumbled loudly.

"Stop that!" said Ferlin severely.

The egg dragged its feet, but at last climbed into its cardboard nest.

Gently, Marthur closed the carton. Everything got quiet. Almost.

"Did you hear that?" Marthur asked.

"What?"

"Scraping. Outside."

"Didn't hear a thing," said Ferlin. She poked inside her ears and muttered, "Did I put those beans back in?"

Marthur was worried. Was somebody out there? Rufus, maybe? Would he spill the beans about the eggs to Dr. Klunk?

Marthur listened closely, holding her breath. Nothing. "Could I say good night to the eggs?" she asked Ferlin.

"Certainl'."

Marthur leaned close to the carton. Twelve times she whispered shyly, "Good night." She heard a dozen mumbled "good nights" in reply and shivered with delight.

"Thanks, Ferlin," said Marthur. "I feel much better."

"Jolly good," said Ferlin. "But remember—don't tell anybody."

"I never would," Marthur promised.

They went their separate ways. It was late and the school was pretty quiet. But a few kids were still straggling around, having a bubble-gum-blowing contest—even though that was against the rules. Marthur wouldn't tell on them. Everything was against the rules at Horace E. Bloggins.

"Hi, Marthur!" the kids yelled between bubbles. "Wanna hang out?"

"Hi!" she called back cheerfully. "I can't. I've got to go see my father!"

Marthur was definitely perked up. *Eggs with legs.* She giggled on her way to the boiler room. Like magic, Marthur had forgotten her troubles—clanking pipes, her mangled name, and Dr. Klunk and Rufus. She had also forgotten about the king.

IV

Marthur never saw her father much; he was so busy doing junk for Dr. Klunk. That made her terribly sad. Their hours rarely crisscrossed. But when they did, the Snapdragons made the most of it. After they gulped supper (in case he had to leave in a rush), Luther read aloud to Marthur (both without earmuffs). He read any story bit he could fit in before some more work came up, hollering over the scronk of the pipes.

Sometimes he stopped reading and bellowed out of the blue, "What's your dream, dear? Apart from wanting bacon, I mean.

What's your utmost fondest most prepos-
terous outlandish wish?"

Marthur would gaze at a picture on the
wall. (With love, Luther Snapdragon tacked
up all of her drawings.)

"I want to be a teacher. Just like Ferlin.
She makes things better for the kids at
Horace E. Bloggins."

Marthur's wish was always the same.

"How I love to hear that," said her father
every time. "It's an unselfish dream—the
very best kind.

"Hold fast to dreams," Luther quoted at
the top of his lungs while the pipes clanked,
"'Cause when dreams go—well, they just go.
A great poet wrote that."

Each time her father said the poem, it
was a bit different. But he always got the
gist.

———

Still thinking about the dancing eggs, Marthur danced through the door and into the boiler room.

"Hello, my sweetheart!" cried Luther Snapdragon above the hiss of the pipes. "Did you have a frabjous day?" (He enjoyed using odd words to entertain her.)

"FRABJOUS!" hollered Marthur. Then they both laughed.

"Can we read, Daddy?" Marthur asked.

"I've only got time for the 'hold fast' poem, then it's back to work." Luther blasted out energetically, "Hold fast to dreams. 'Cause if dreams run, life is like having—uh— no sun! A great poet wrote that."

"I know," Marthur yelled, "a *very* great poet!"

"What's your dream, dear?" Luther asked.

"To be a teacher. Just like Ferlin," said Marthur. "Daddy, what's *your* dream?"

"For your dream to come true. Well, gotta go!"

Luther kissed her on the top of the head (in a hollow spot where she'd cut some gum out).

"Hold fast, my dumpling!"

"Hold fast, Daddy!"

Luther Snapdragon hadn't been gone long when—*wham! wham! wham!*—a frightful pounding rattled the sweltering boiler room. Marthur had put her earmuffs on while she did her homework. But the racket was so loud, she still heard it. (And felt it.) Suddenly, a length of old pipe slumped like a log on a fire. She braced herself for the whole place to cave in.

But nothing collapsed on her. The sound was coming from only one spot. Somebody was pummeling the door! (Luckily, she'd locked it.)

"Who is it?" she yelled.

"Rufus, you doofus!"

Marthur's stomach dropped. What in the name of all that was horrible was *he* doing there? Why wasn't he home? And why would he come to Marthur's, of all places?

May as well be the big bad wolf, Marthur thought. She held her breath and waited for him to huff and puff and blow the whole place down.

"What do you want?" She tried to sound brave, but her voice was shaking.

"I WANT THOSE DANCING EGGS!"

V

Marthur's legs quivered like jelly. Her head spun. The dancing eggs were a secret between her and Ferlin!

"What did you say? You want to dance?" she shouted at Rufus, hoping she'd heard him wrong.

"In your dreams, brain-o! I want the eggs!"

So…She hadn't imagined that scraping sound outside Ferlin's classroom. It was Rufus the rat, spying for Dr. Klunk.

"*Which* eggs?" Marthur stalled like mad. "Ferlin's got goose eggs and tortoise eggs and platypus eggs and hummingbird eggs and eel eggs and grouse eggs and louse eggs and snake eggs and steak eggs and—"

"Shut your stupid egg-a-thon up!" Rufus hollered. "Anyways, there's no such thing as steak eggs."

"Where do you think steaks come from?" Marthur blathered on.

"Don't mess with me, smarty-pants. I mean the eggs your precious Ferlin pulled from her purse. I've got a plan for those little hoofers!"

"What gophers?" Marthur shrieked. "I don't know what you're talking about!"

"Yeah, right!" Rufus roared back. "Get 'em or I'll pulverize—" Rufus stopped. He had a better idea. "Get 'em or we'll dump over every trash can in school!"

Marthur groaned, imagining mounds of garbage everywhere.

"Your daddy'll look like a slacker and

lose his job. Then you'll be in the street—and you'll stop buggin' me!"

"Me bug YOU? You're *crazy*!"

"Shut your face and get the eggs from that science freak!"

"No!" Marthur yelled frantically. "They're Ferlin's!"

"Tough tarantulas! I want 'em! An' I want 'em TOMORROW!"

Marthur gasped. "But *how*?"

"You're so *smart*, figure it out."

"I CAN'T!"

"Swipe 'em, brain-o!"

Then Marthur remembered the king. She was desperate, so she hollered out, "The king is coming—and he's going to get you!"

"A king! Man, you'll try *anything*!" Rufus cackled like a lunatic hen. "Now get those eggs, or Daddy's had it!"

Marthur heard him scuttle away. Ferlin's

words rang in her ears: "But remember—don't tell anybody."

Marthur was aghast. *She'll think I told Rufus! Ferlin trusts me. How can I steal from her? But if I don't…*

Marthur's world was falling to pieces. She'd lost her name. She was about to become a thief and lose her friend Ferlin. For some crazy reason, Rufus hated her. Even if she got the dancing eggs, he was rotten enough to dump the trash, anyway. Then her father would be bogged down with more work—or he'd lose his job and they'd be on the street. On top of everything else, from shouting she had a sore throat. It was too much. A king couldn't help her. Nobody could. Marthur threw herself onto her cot and sobbed.

The next morning Marthur woke up wanting to urp. She'd hardly slept a smidgen.

Dumped-over trash cans and stolen eggs got scrambled up in her nightmares. She was torn in two. What should she do about the little dancers? And what about her father?

Luther Snapdragon had always told her, "Blood's thicker than soup." Now, crumpled on her rumpled cot, she knew what he meant: Family comes first. She had to stick by her father—and steal from her teacher.

Maybe a king really *was* coming. But she just couldn't wait for such a far-fetched thing. She'd steal Ferlin's key from Luther's master set and snatch the eggs when Ferlin wasn't there. Just one teensy problem: The watchful griffin would probably eat her. Yikes! She'd have to heist them from under Ferlin's nose!

Little by little, Marthur hatched a plan. She'd snitch the dancing eggs during science class.

VI

It took Marthur a while to work out her plan, so class had already begun when she slouched into the room, hunched under her father's heavy dark coat. Her own was too raggedy and small to cover up stolen eggs. She looked like somebody wearing her own shadow.

Ferlin had just launched a small rocket fueled with cranberry juice. The rocket sizzled around the ceiling. All eyes were fixed on it. All but Marthur's. She pretended to spit her gum into the wastebasket while she looked all around. The eggs were nowhere in sight! Of course, Ferlin wouldn't just leave them out for somebody to pick up. Maybe break. Where *were* they?

Marthur stooped down, fumbling like she'd missed the wastebasket. And—what was this?—on the handle of a small cupboard, she saw the selfsame design as on the egg carton: that funny old spoon. She gave the handle a little tug, and—oh my!—it opened. Inside the cupboard was the purple carton.

Slowly—so slowly—she placed one hand on it. Marthur nearly stopped breathing. What if the eggs yelled for help? (If they could say good night, they could scream bloody murder.) She had to take that chance.

Trembling, she sneaked a peek at Ferlin. With a ruler (which looked a lot like a wand) the teacher was urging the rocket onward in a blast of rainbow stars. It surged around the light fixtures and began orbiting one. Ferlin watched in scientific triumph, oblivious to Marthur.

Suddenly, Marthur got the sweats. Ferlin *knew*. Ferlin always knew. Heart thumping and cartonless, Marthur raced back to her desk.

All day she festered. During recess she searched for a colorful bird or a beautiful blossom—the slightest sign that things would be okay. She saw some nice stuff. But the fact remained: As soon as she stole those dancing eggs (and she had to), she'd be a thief.

At noon everybody in the whole school was stuffed into the lunchroom, creating a fabulous hullabaloo. The little kids were eating pretty nicely. The older ones gobbled. Rufus and the bruisers were done eating. They were cruising for trouble.

Rufus grabbed a gob of paper-covered straws. "Watch me, guys!" He dipped a straw in somebody's mashed potatoes, blew like crazy, and shot the wrapper to the ceiling. The paper stuck. "WHOOPEE!" Rufus roared.

Rufus's minions grabbed straws, loaded them with potatoes, and shot the wrappers at the ceiling. Soon wrappers and wrappers and wrappers hung down like flimsy little stalactites. The rest of the kids just gawked.

"I'm gettin' Klunk!" Rufus yelled at them. "I'm telling what you guys did!" He and his rowdies scuttled away. Their laughter rang in the halls.

What were the kids going to do? They couldn't get the straw wrappers down. Klunk was going to blame them for the mess. Marthur was sitting with her friends, eating a peanut butter sandwich (with no peanut butter). Suddenly, she spronged up. She knew where her father kept a ladder. In a flash she hauled it out, scrambled up, and yanked the papers down. Two fifth graders held the ladder for her.

Then—zippo!—Marthur stashed the ladder and scooted to her seat. She put a finger to her lips. The kids sat like sphinxes, waiting.

Klunk roared in, his spies behind him. "Okay," he blustered. "Number facts for a week for this little straw caper!" (He didn't know any number facts; that didn't matter.)

"What caper?" The kids started buzzing, looking puzzled.

Klunk pointed a fat finger at the ceiling. "That—" He nearly choked. "Rufus, you moron! You *oxy*-moron! There's nothing up there!" He spluttered and stalked out. All the kids glanced at Marthur. They clapped—silently.

"Hey, brain-o!" Rufus bellowed louder than usual. He was burned. He couldn't figure what had just happened, but he suspected Marthur. "You said you'd share your lunch with me. *Eggs*. Remember?"

He stood by a trash can, tipping it farther, farther, farther....

"Don't do that!" Marthur screamed. "You'll get them. After school."

"I better."

VII

School was out. Kids were streaming from the dark brick corridors of Horace E. Bloggins like trails of noisy ants. Some were already biking away. Some were waiting (noisily) for the buses. By now most of them had seen the carving with the bizarre prediction about a king. "Are you the king?" a boy asked his friend. "I don't think so," said the other boy, feeling his head for a crown. They laughed.

Last chance to filch the eggs. Marthur had a headache from worrying. Ferlin was going to hate her. But what could Marthur do? She had to keep her father out of trouble.

She hurried to the science room, the big coat flopping like a hound's loose skin. But on her way, she heard yelling. Bugged by the straw-paper incident, Dr. Klunk was making some first graders nail Jell-O to a tree. (Dr. Klunk didn't like first graders—or trees.) "The Jell-O stays put or you're doing laps, people! Fifty big ones! Now start nailing!" he hollered gleefully.

Marthur glanced over. The first graders were trying to swing at the nails, but they could barely lift the hammers. The Jell-O jiggled through their fingers and plopped to the ground before they could get a nail near it. Some of the kids were already dragging around the track, crying and crying. Marthur needed the eggs—NOW. But she couldn't stand watching the poor kids suffer.

"STOP!" she shouted. "I'll do the laps—for all of them!"

Dr. Klunk brightened. If Marthur ran all

the laps (he couldn't figure out how many, but he knew it would be a lot), she'd collapse on the track. That would be excellent to watch.

"Hop to it, little missy! The rest of you get lost!"

Marthur's mind spun, trying to think of a way out. She crossed her fingers. "I've got a doctor appointment," she fibbed, and felt horrible. "But I'll do double—tomorrow."

Klunk stared at her from behind his wraparound shades. "Make my day." He grinned.

Marthur heaved a huge sigh of relief and dashed for the science room. She knew Ferlin would still be there. She always stayed late.

"Hi, Ferlin," she said limply.

"Hello, Marthur," said Ferlin, bebangled with outlandish jewelry. "Something on your mind?"

Marthur got flustered. She couldn't very well say, "I'm gonna steal your dancing eggs." She had to distract her—so she blurted, "I want to be a teacher! That's my dream." She added, "Hold fast to dreams 'cause they are broken birds."

"An unusual sentiment," remarked Ferlin.

"It's a famous poem that means don't quit on stuff," Marthur said. "I won't quit on teaching. Will you show me how?"

"I was wondering when you were going to ask," Ferlin said mysteriously.

"You knew about my dream?"

"Since kindergarten."

Marthur gaped. Finally she said, "So. Will you teach me?"

"Now?"

"Yes—please." While Ferlin taught, she was in another world. She absolutely riveted on a topic and noticed nothing else. Once she got going, Marthur could easily snatch the eggs.

"Teaching is the finest job there is," said Ferlin vigorously. "I would be *overjoyed* to show you its intricacies. But I'm on my way home. Instruction starts tomorrow."

"OH NO!" Marthur yelped.

"What?"

"I—er—needtosharpenmypencil!"

"Go ahead. I'll get my things."

Marthur rushed to the little cupboard with the weird spoon symbol on it. She fake-cranked the pencil sharpener like mad, keeping a wild eye on Ferlin. The second Ferlin's head was turned, Marthur opened the cupboard, whisked out the purple carton, and bundled it under her sloppy coat.

"Marthur…," Ferlin said slowly, peering from under her bushy eyebrows.

Help! I'm caught! Marthur thought, feeling lower than a dirt-digging worm.

"Would you snap off the light?"

Marthur nearly fainted. "Uh—sure."

"Same time tomorrow, first teaching lesson." Ferlin sparkled merrily as they went out. "Till then, 'Hold fast to dreams'!"

Her heart thumping nearly through her chest, Marthur held fast to the stolen eggs.

VIII

In a panic Marthur lurched along the dim corridor, clutching her father's coat closed. She could feel the eggs jiggling inside the carton. And she was almost certain she heard them giggling.

Marthur's brain buzzed. Her very first teaching lesson was the next day. She should have felt like floating; instead she felt heavy as lead. *What have I done?* she thought. *I've burgled! I'm a thief! A crook! I'm as horrid as Rufus and Dr. Klunk!*

Then she worried, *Ferlin knows. I know she knows. She always knows everything—even before it happens. "Hold fast to dreams." Right. Now*

Ferlin will never teach me to teach. Even if I do learn, what teacher would filch magic eggs? A good teacher would never do such a thing! And what about Daddy? Klunk will find out what I've done, and he'll be out of a job!

Marthur spun around. "I have to take them back!" she said out loud, running toward Ferlin's room.

"*That'll* happen," sneered Rufus, pouncing from a dark doorway. "Give 'em over or we'll pound you to jelly!"

He was surrounded by his meatball minions. They usually hung around after school to see if there were any kids left to pester. But this time they'd been hanging around waiting for Marthur.

"You don't *really* want them," Marthur said, nonchalant outside, inside a total quiver.

"I really *do*. I'm gonna charge people

oodles to watch 'em dance their little legs off. Even though I'm a kid, I'll be RICH. Then I won't have to get good grades like you, brain-o. That'll show my dad—"

"Show him what?"

"None o' yer beeswax, Einstein!"

"Why do you hate me?" Marthur blurted. "I never did anything to you."

"Yeah? You do everything *right*, you—you—BRAIN-O!"

Rufus grabbed the carton, tore it open, and set the eggs on the edge of a ledge.

"Dance!" he snarled.

The eggs lay there on their gleaming white sides, their small shoes shining like black jelly beans.

"*Dance!*" Rufus yelled.

Not a wiggle. Not a jiggle.

"DANCE!"

"They're the wrong eggs," Marthur said

in desperation. "I made a mistake." (Now she was a liar, too.)

"Right, nimble-wit. That's why they got feet." Rufus gave the eggs a hard-boiled glare.

"Ya won't dance?" he fumed. His Big Plan was squelched. "Maybe you're good for something else—like *eating*. Come on, guys, let's cook the Dirty Dozen!"

Marthur screamed, "You can't do that!"

"Why not?"

"If you do, you won't get rich!"

"These lazy eggs aren't worth a dime, anyways!"

"But it's—it's—*murder*."

"They're eggs, brain-o!" Rufus roared. "But since you care so much, you get to watch me boil 'em. In the *boiler* room!" He laughed and snorty-snorted, like a pig.

Rufus shoved Marthur along in front of him. As she stumbled home, Marthur racked her brain about what she'd done to make him hate her. And she racked her brain for a way to save Ferlin's eggs.

It's all my fault, she thought. *Think fast or the little dancers are goners!*

IX

Marthur was undone. A waterwall of tears welled behind her eyes, but she wouldn't let Rufus see them. When they reached the boiler room, she fumbled with the doorknob, hoping to dart in quickly and slam the door on the hooligans.

"Get a move on, fumblethumbs," snorted Rufus. "We've got cooking to do. The Dirty Dozen's goin' DOWN!"

Luther Snapdragon opened the door.

"Daddy!" The tears nearly gushed.

"Come in, everybody!" yelled Luther Snapdragon enthusiastically, removing his earmuffs. "It's always nice to see Martha's friends!" (He, of course, called her by her real name.)

Rufus and his pals swarmed in.

"Nice pipes!" Rufus shouted with fake politeness, seeing the ancient steam heater.

"Thank you, young man!" replied Luther Snapdragon, as the heater kronked and hissed.

"They have to go, Daddy!" cried Marthur urgently.

"They just arrived! And welcome they are!" stated Luther heartily.

"But, Daddy, it's *Rufus*! He's going to boil eggs!"

Marthur was jumping up and down as if fleas were nipping her legs.

"Eggs-cellent!" Luther Snapdragon joked. "The water's ready! I was boiling it for coffee!"

"Eggs-cellent!" Rufus grinned.

"Nothing tastier than a-negg!" shouted Luther with gusto. "Martha and I favor poached."

Marthur was about to pop. Her father didn't know about Rufus because she hadn't told him. If she had, no doubt he would have smiled and spouted his solution to everything: "Hold fast, my dear! Show them you're a Snapdragon!"

"Mr. Snapdragon!" Rufus shouted, all smarmy. "I sure admire your daughter's brains!" To Luther, Rufus seemed to be a nice young fellow.

"She *is* quite bright!" yelled Luther with pride. (Marthur's photo was often in the local newspaper; she won lots of prizes at Horace E. Bloggins.)

Luther Snapdragon glanced at Rufus's (stolen) watch. "Oh, my word! Dr. Klunk wants me right now. Gotta go. Cheerio! Hold fast!"

"DADDY! WAIT!" Marthur yelled after him. But her throat was still sore from the night before. So the words scraped out in squeaks.

"Daddy can't help you now, megamind!" Rufus taunted. "Let's get to it!"

In a wink the Dirty Dozen were awash with water in a pot on top of a pipe. Steam clouded. The pipe hissed. The water burbled.

Rufus rubbed his hands together. "This is what you get for wrecking my plan! You won't dance, you lose, chumps!" He smirked at the twelve white lumps.

The water boiled faster. It roiled and rolled quite jollily—like in an old-time cauldron.

"STOP!" Marthur yelled. *"You're killing them!"* She flailed at the pot, hoping to dump it over. But the minions grabbed her first.

Marthur nearly dissolved. But she didn't. She stuck her chin out instead.

"Isn't cooking a gas?" Rufus gloated. "You're the Marthur Stewart (rhymes with *blooert*) of Horace E. Bloggins!"

The eggs thudded against one another like small stones. Strange sounds erupted from them. Suddenly—*crrrr-ick! crrrr-ock! crrrr-eek!*—they cracked open.

"Criminy!" Rufus screamed.

A dozen tiny dragons gleamed in the boiling water, eyes lit with devilment, hissing their heads off. And they were clawing their way out.

X

The dragons roared from the rim of the pot:

> *"Cook us in bug juice!*
> *Char us in oil!*
> *Fry us in Brylcreem!*
> *Bake us in soil!*
> *Braise us in soy sauce!*
> *Give it a whoil!*
> *The hotter the better!*
> *We love to boil!"*

Their eyes spurted sparks of burning green. Their scales blazed like leaves aflame.

They belched (loudly) fireballs like Roman candles.

Marthur was delighted. The eggs were *alive*—and transformed!

"Hurrah for the dragons!" she croaked.

"Duck!" yelled Rufus. A surging fireball singed his baseball cap.

The scaly creatures scrambled free. They prowled along the pipes, pawing the Snap-dragons' laundry, hissing and hurling fire-balls and smoke bombs at will. (They paused now and then to chortle bloodthirstily.)

The boiler room turned to chaos. Pande-monium. Bedlam. A total hullabaloo.

"We're cooked!" roared Rufus, scared out of his skull.

"We'll be torched! Scorched! Blistered! Burnt to a crisp! Toast!" shrieked his gang. They were too rattled to dash for the door. They scrunched themselves into corners like roaches and whimpered.

Marthur was surprised to realize that she wasn't frightened. In fact, she felt pretty calm. Her father's slogan rang in her head: *Show them you're a Snapdragon!*

She pulled herself up to look as tall as she possibly could (about four feet). "Dragons!" Marthur shouted over the din. "My father's old! He works to the bone! He'll be pretty upset to come home to this mess. You're having lots of fun. But stop, *please*!" Her mind raced. Even if the dragons relented, how could she ever clean up? (At least she didn't have to do laundry; they'd burned that.) Her voice quivered a little, but she held fast—a Snapdragon at her best.

Marthur's words slowed the dragons down a bit. But they were too full of razzmatazz to quit.

"CEASE AND DESIST THESE PYRO-TECHNIC ANTICS!" thundered a furious voice.

At once the dragons ceased and desisted charring the premises. They went stiff—except for their mischievous glittering eyes.

"Ferlin!" cried Marthur. "Thank goodness!"

"Run for it!" screeched Rufus. "I've seen her in action. She's a witch!"

"The proper term is *wizard*!" snapped Ferlin.

The boys hotfooted it away. As they shot past, the dragons spouted sparks at the seats of their pants. Rufus turned back to yell, "Wait till Klunk hears that Daddy's dragons are trashing school property!"

Whang! Marthur slammed the door in his pinched-in weevil face. She looked at the devastation, then at Ferlin.

"Funny!" Marthur shouted. "In spite of everything, I feel good!"

"Slamming doors has that effect!"

"Are you really a lizard like you told Rufus?" Marthur asked.

"*Wizard.*"

"But I thought wizards were—"

"Men? Oh *my*, no. Some of the greats are women."

"Are you one of the greats?"

"Let's just say I have a certain… Reputation."

Ferlin raised a hand and commanded, "Aroint thee! Out! Begone!" With that, the smoke sucked itself out the door. All signs of havoc vanished. "As you were," Ferlin ordered the dragons.

With a clashing of claws and a flurry of shell shards, once again they were eggs.

"And put on your shoes."

Grumbling, the eggs obeyed. Then they hopped back into the purple carton—the carton decorated with the weird old spoon.

"That settles that," Ferlin said, dusting ashes from her hair.

"Sorry about the eggs." Tears glazed Marthur's eyes. "I didn't want—"

"I know what happened," said Ferlin gently.

"Ferlin?" said Marthur, still shaky.

"Yes?"

"Can't you use your—er—*special techniques* to nicen-up Klunk and Rufus?"

"I'm afraid not, Marthur. People must change by themselves. Tricks don't count," Ferlin said. "Well, don't forget our little class tomorrow. After school." Then, her handbag bulky with dragon eggs, she swooped out.

"Good night," Marthur whispered.

She thought she heard "Good night" float back.

The eggs were safe. And the next day (Hold fast!) she'd learn how to teach.

Marthur should have slept well. But she kept hearing Rufus's threat: *"Wait till Klunk hears that Daddy's dragons are trashing school property!"*

Even though the boiler room was clean again, Marthur knew her troubles weren't over. Why couldn't that weird saying be true? Why couldn't there *really* be a king on the way to Horace E. Bloggins School?

XI

Open up, Snapdragon!" A sharp shout shattered the morning.

"Dr. Klunk!" yelped Marthur, leaping up from her cot. She dashed to open the door, hoping to hustle Klunk away before he woke up her father.

"Good morning, Dr. Klunk," Marthur greeted him sweetly (but loudly—because of the pipes).

The way he snarled at her, you'd think she'd said, "Rotten day to you, you old canker."

Dr. Klunk glared like a gargoyle through his wraparounds. Rufus Turk slouched beside him (without his minions for once). He was one big smirk.

"Don't you dare 'Good morning' me, little missy," Klunk stormed. "The word is out, the king is coming. The king? POOP! *I'm* in charge here. Clean up this place! And cough up those dragons! I can control 'em if anybody can! I'll show the interloper that we don't need him!" He buffaloed his way in, Rufus swaggering in his wake.

Then Rufus stopped short. He gawped. "I don't get it. Where's the dragons? Where's the smoke? Where's the total DEVASTATION?"

Luther Snapdragon woke up and coughed.

"Little case of smoke inhalation?" snapped Klunk.

"Smoke?" asked Luther Snapdragon, grogged with sleep. "No, thanks." (He was highly against cigars and cigarettes.)

"From the *dragons*!" Klunk ranted. "You savage! You've blatantly allowed them to deface school property!"

"Dragons?" Luther sat bolt upright, flabbergasted.

"No use playacting. Your name's not Snap*dragon* for nothing," Klunk puffed, pleased at making that connection.

"He's innocent!" cried Marthur. "And he needs his rest. Can't you see—there are no dragons. And no defacing."

"There *were*! And there was smoke and fire!" bellowed Rufus. "I swear!" (Unfortunately, he swore a lot.)

"Where's the proof?" asked Marthur.

Klunk snorted. "I'm the principal. I don't need proof!"

"But there's nothing *wrong*," Marthur insisted.

"Maybe there is. And maybe there isn't."

Klunk glared. "I'll talk to that Ferlin woman next. Rufus informed me you're in cahoots."

"Cahoots!" Luther was aghast.

"Pipe down, Snapdragon! You're on probation!"

"Probation!" cried Marthur. "That's not fair!"

"Fair, shmair," Klunk sneered.

Luther Snapdragon asked nervously, "Can I still work?"

"Don't miss a minute—or you'll be on SUSPENSION!"

When the intruders were gone, Luther Snapdragon said in his usual cloudy way, "What's all this about savages and kings?" Then he asked gently, "Martha, dear, do you have something to tell me?"

"Yes, Daddy," she replied truthfully. "But first I've got to warn Ferlin to hide the dragons!"

XII

In the science room there was a telephone. And a red baboon. And a picture of—George Washington. And there were three antbears sitting on chairs. And two little lizards. And a pair of gizzards. And a unicorn brush. And a sink full of mush.

"Good *night*!" cried Dr. Klunk, jostling past some early pupils. "What a room!"

The griffin was enjoying its morning ration of figs. It statued itself immediately when Klunk blammed in. Klunk shoved the griffin aside and roared up to Ferlin.

Marthur tore in after him. "Ferlin! They're coming! Hide the—"

Pwoff! She plowed into Dr. Klunk, nearly knocking off his shades.

"Hide the what?" Klunk growled.

Marthur thought fast. "Onions!"

"Yeah, *right,*" snarled Rufus. He stood glued to the principal, like a nasty little shadow.

"Hide the onions!" proclaimed Ferlin. "The slightest exposure to light might utterly spoil our class experiment!"

"Never mind onions! My sources say you have fire-breathing *dragons* in your possession!" Klunk stated like the gasbag he was. "I'm confiscating them! No more flaming around! No more scorching! I can keep things as shipshape as anybody. The king may be coming, but *I* don't need him!"

"Dragons?" said Ferlin. "Amazing."

"She's faking," rasped Rufus. "I saw 'em. They burnt my pants. Look!"

Rufus always wore the same pair of jeans. He knew the proof was there, right on his rear. Klunk checked that and roared, "What singe, you little rodent?"

Rufus pretzeled himself to look.

Marthur giggled.

"What's so funny?"

"Your jeans just turned plaid."

Rufus's eyes flared like matches. His face got splotchy with fury. "My singe! My jeans!" he screamed. "Turn 'em back!"

He jostled Marthur and hissed, "This ain't over yet, Miss Special Class. Me an' the guys'll be outside…" The threat hung in the air like a bunched fist. Then Rufus bolted, muttering, "Plaid!" Like it was the worst curse word in the world.

"Dragons. I don't recall any," mused Ferlin, getting back to the larger problem. Klunk didn't wait for permission. He began ransacking Ferlin's stuff with gusto. He'd show any king who happened by just who controlled things at Bloggins.

Klunk dug about like a truffle pig. Marthur watched nervously. Uh-oh!—she spotted the dragon-egg carton (still smudged with soot from the night before). Marthur gasped in horror. Dr. Klunk was so close, he could sneeze on the carton! Now Ferlin was really in for it!

Marthur had to distract him. "Hold this," she said, shoving one of Ferlin's hedge-hogs at him.

Klunk held it gingerly, as if it were a tiny spiny football.

"Hey, little missy!" he shouted at Marthur. "Whaddya think you're doing?" Then he stopped stock-still. "Go to the bathroom at once!" he yelled.

"But I don't have to."

"You *do* have to! I need paper towels! The KING is coming any minute and look what this—this—creature has done!"

The hedgehog had peed on Dr. Klunk.

Marthur glanced at Ferlin. "Can you do without me?" she asked.

"We will be fine."

"What about the—" Marthur stared wildly at the egg carton.

"I'll see to them. After all, *you're going to need them later*," Ferlin said.

Marthur felt stupefied. "What do you mean?"

"I mean what I mean. Now go. *We will be fine.*"

But I won't be, Marthur thought. She knew Rufus and his gang were waiting for her. Still, she had no choice.

Marthur gulped and went out.

XIII

Yo, brain-o!" Rufus hooted. "Wait up!" He and the minions poured from the gloomy hallway.

As *if*! Marthur took off. Not only was she smart, she was also a pretty fast runner. She spurted into high gear. She sprinted as though ten thousand demons were snapping at her heels. (Really, there were only six.)

The boys stampeded after her, yelling like wild apes. Once Marthur looked back fast and nearly whiplashed herself. They were still rumbling close behind, their sneakers squeaking like anything.

Marthur turned a corner and zipped through a door.

"Safe—for now," she panted. "Those guys wouldn't be caught *dead* in the girls' bathroom."

Marthur was pooped from running. Pooped from worrying. About her father. And Ferlin. And Rufus. And the dragons (which Dr. Klunk had probably already found). And the teaching lessons (which would probably never happen). She would have loved nothing better than to collapse on the bathroom floor, her cheek pressed against the cool tiles. But the paper towels! Dr. Klunk was waiting.

Before going back, Marthur turned on the tap and doused herself with cold water. She felt a speck better. She grabbed a gob of paper towels, took a deep breath, and prepared to run for it.

Just then, for some uncanny reason,

Marthur glanced at the wall to the left of the towel dispenser. Two seconds before, there'd been nothing there. But then, there it was. From nowhere, it had just *appeared*.

Something bizarre was sticking out from the tile. It was a long pink tongue.

XIV

Marthur froze. The big tongue just hung there, glowing with a peculiar pink tinge. A bloodred stone was lodged in it like a great big cough drop. And where the tongue got skinny, there were lots of gems and strange scratchings, like writing.

"Gol-*leeee!*" Marthur yelled. It was so bedazzling, she had to shield her eyes.

Little dragons were one thing. Marthur could see them and knew what she was dealing with. But a big weird tongue? Her imagination went nuts. *What's attached to this thing? What if it's connected to a monster that's about to burst through the wall and start slurping up kids? Jeez!*

"You're a Snapdragon," she reminded herself. But she couldn't save the whole school from the monster in the wall. (It was hard enough saving them from Klunk.) Still, she had to warn everybody!

Marthur shot out of there like a cannonball. Even if they'd still been lying in ambush, Rufus and his scruffians couldn't have caught her. She sped as fast as a polished pig. (Maybe faster.)

"A HEE-NOR-MOUS TONGUE!" Marthur hollered as she hurtled down the hall.

"What are you blatting about?" Dr. Klunk came clumping around a corner. Marthur had taken so long, he'd come to give her a few hundred demerits. She was so startled, she dropped the paper towels. They fluttered down like limp brown leaves.

"A tongue! A m-m-monster's one," Marthur stammered. *"In the w-w-wall of the girls' bathroom!"*

Klunk didn't believe her. But he had to check it out—in case the king (ridiculous!) was really coming.

"From hedgehog pee to giant tongues! A principal's work is never done!" Klunk groused. "Don't just stand there. Let's go!"

"Where?"

"To the office, of course. I need backup."

Marthur scrambled after him. "Don't you need paper towels?"

"THAT dried up, you took so long, little missy. When this tongue business is over, I'll slap you with enough demerits to keep you in detention for the rest of your life!"

"What about the dragons?" Marthur asked nervously. "Did you—find them?"

"I found a purple egg carton—empty. That Ferlin's as slippery as a greased eel."

Marthur nearly collapsed with relief. Then she felt silly. Ferlin was a wizard. She had tamed *dragons*. Turned them back into eggs. Cleaned the boiler room in a finger-snap. She didn't need Marthur to save her from anything.

With Marthur at his heels, Dr. Klunk scrugged into his office and yelled at his secretary, Miss Tweezers (rhymes with *sneezers*). "Get Snapdragon! Tell him to get over here pronto, chop-chop, ASAP, on the double! And to bring a golf club! We've got trouble!"

Miss Tweezers called Luther on her walkie-talkie and reported back. "He's only got a broom."

"Well, he jolly well better bring it! *Anything* could happen!"

Pretty soon Luther Snapdragon reeled in. He was so weary from overwork, he wobbled.

"Follow me," Dr. Klunk snapped. "We're after a tongue!"

"I see," Luther Snapdragon said blearily. (But he didn't.)

Marthur hugged her father—and propped him up.

"I love you, Daddy," she said. "Please be supercareful."

"Cut the fond adieus, little missy," hissed Klunk. "*You're* coming with us. You're leading the way!"

XV

They hustled to the bathroom, Marthur in front, Luther Snapdragon next, brandishing his broom, gentle though he was. (Guess who was last?)

"Hey," said Klunk. "This is the *boys'* bathroom."

Marthur was astounded. Flabbergasted. Amazed. Dumbfounded.

No wonder Rufus hadn't found her. Who'd look in there for a girl?

"Oops." Marthur blushed to the tips of her ears.

"A girl in the boys' bathroom! That's a blot on your permanent record," Klunk shot.

The tongue was waiting for them. Doubtless expecting the worst, Klunk shoved Marthur in first.

"Brace up," her father whispered. "Look to the positive. Maybe it's a friendly tongue."

"Okay, Daddy," said Marthur, though jangled with fear. Then they tiptoed in.

"There it is." Marthur pointed, shielding her eyes from its flare.

"Watch it," Klunk hissed from a safe distance. "It could be dangerous."

It was dim in the boys' bathroom. Slowly, warily, Marthur and her father sneaked closer. Luther held the broom at the ready. They looked harder—and sighed with relief, like air whooshing out of two giant punctured balloons.

The tongue wasn't dangerous. In fact, it wasn't a tongue at all. It was an old handle. A *very* old handle. (Maybe the oldest handle in the world.) It was wedged deep into the cold masonry of the boys' bathroom of Horace E. Bloggins School.

"Well?" snarled Klunk from way far back.

"It's just a handle!" the Snapdragons chimed together.

Klunk immediately muscled himself in front to see.

The ancient handle was WONDROUS STRANGE. Fantastic. It was hammered of solid gold that shone with the pink glow of the ages. A colossal ruby (not a cough drop) flamed at its widest expanse; diamonds and emeralds and sapphires and amethysts and aquamarines and opals and topazes and tigereyes encrusted the rest—except for where the old-fashioned writing was.

Marthur's mouth dropped open. She recognized the handle! It was part of the emblem on Ferlin's egg carton!

Dr. Klunk and Luther Snapdragon and Marthur peered closely. They squinted like mad. The mysterious, spidery letters declared:

Whoso Pulleth This Spoon
from This Wall
Is Rightwise King of All Bloggins.

"Well, I'll be a star-spangled banner!" Klunk blazed.

His eyes glazed with excitement. Marthur could see them burning behind his dark glasses. Klunk yelled, "Rufus, I know you and those nincompoops are out there! Stand guard! Nobody comes in!"

"Sure thing!" Rufus yelled from where he was lurking.

"Stand back, you two! Give me room!" Klunk ordered, seething like an overloaded socket. "I'm going to yank this spoon out! I AM THE KING!" he screamed. Like the guy who sells mattresses on TV.

Marthur and her father gaped at Klunk, horrorized. Klunk gripped the spoon handle. The ruby gazed at him like a big red eye. He pulled.

Nothing happened, except he slipped and—*oof!*—went sprawling. Klunk struggled up and tugged again. Zilch. The spoon remained rooted like a great gold tooth.

"Must be some sort of test," muttered Klunk. (He'd never passed a test without cheating in his life.)

He wedged one foot against the tile for leverage and strained like an ox. His neck swelled. His collar got tight. His eyes bulged. His face turned blue. A button popped.

"Come out, you stupid utensil!" By then

he was pretty mad. He was sweating like a pig, and the jewels had scraped his pudgy hands.

But the spoon stayed stuck.

"A real gut-buster," Luther Snapdragon remarked.

Klunk yelled, "Don't just stand there, you two! Get out! Do some homework! Go sweep something!"

"Yes, sir," replied the Snapdragons.

"WAIT!" Klunk's shout echoed like a cheap brass bell. "This spoon is TOP SECRET." (It wouldn't be for long, when he told Rufus.)

He yanked off one shoe and slid his smelly sock over the handle as a flimsy disguise. (As if one reeking sock could throw anybody off the scent.)

"Don't tell a soul," Klunk warned again, *"if you know what's good for you."*

There was nothing more to do there. The Snapdragons slogged down the hall. Marthur slumped.

"Jolly up, dear," said her father. "Look to the positive. Dr. Klunk doesn't have the spoon."

"Yet."

XVI

The rest of the day moved along slowly, like a river of mud. Only Marthur's body was in class; her mind was on the spoon in the bathroom wall. At least part of it was. The rest of her mind was on her first teaching lesson, which was coming after school.

Marthur must have checked the clock a hundred times at least. But that made the time completely creep.

FINALLY school was over. Marthur raced for Ferlin's room.

"Just a red-hot minute, little missy!" Dr. Klunk roared in her ear. "You've got laps to run, remember?"

OH NO! The Jell-O laps! No way would Klunk let her off again. So Marthur dragged out to the track and started jogging. Around and around. To keep from crying, she kept saying, "You're a Snapdragon. You're a Snapdragon." Somehow that got her through—that and the thought that she was saving the first graders.

At last Marthur finished. Night was coming. The lights in the corridors were already on. No other kids were around. Slowly, she dragged to Ferlin's room. (She couldn't race; she was too pooped.)

"Hold fast!" Marthur told herself, though she didn't have much hope that Ferlin had waited so long. Maybe she wouldn't want to teach her at all, Marthur was so late.

Sure enough, the lights were out. Marthur's heart dropped. She'd lost her chance. But just in case, she squinted through the window. Maybe Ferlin was doing an experiment in the dark.

The instant she looked, the blank chalkboard began pulsing with a greenish light like it was lit from inside. A message appeared on the chalkboard:

> Attention, Marthur.
> Change of schedule.
> Come back tomorrow.

Marthur was so happy, she nearly cried.

She went home dazed and confused. What was the ancient spoon all about? Why was it the same as the one on the egg carton? And why had Ferlin said that Marthur was going to need the dragons? Nobody needed dragons. Nobody even *believed* in dragons. *Ferlin must be losing her mind.*

By the time Marthur got to the boiler

room, her father had gone to work. He had left her a cheerful note:

Dearest Martha,
    Off to the salt mines.
Speaking of salt, there are three grains left for your egg.
    Poach it up!
    Love, Daddy
    P.S. Don't worry about the TOP SECRET.

Marthur *couldn't* "poach it up"—what if it were a dragon egg? Anyhow, she was too stressed to eat. Probably right then, Dr. Klunk was prizing the wondrous spoon from the bathroom wall. Probably the next day he'd be king. Then the kids at Bloggins would *really* be at his mercy! (And he didn't have any.)

King Klunk. Not even King Kong would be worse.

XVII

A juicy rumor spreads itself. But as soon as Rufus found out about the spoon, he nudged that story along.

The next day, on her way to class, Marthur overheard the buzz: "Whoso pulleth this spoon from this wall is rightwise king of all Bloggins."

She nearly screamed, *"Everybody knows! Daddy and I will be blamed for telling!"* She imagined the two of them huddled in a cardboard box in a dingy alley, snow peltering around their ears, and nearly burst into tears.

It didn't take long for kids to begin trickling out of science class. Some said they had the flu. They doubled over and held their bellies and looked fake urpy. Some squirmed and pretended they urgently needed to go to the bathroom. (They did, Marthur knew—to wrench at that spoon.) Everybody wanted to be king.

One kid said he could hear his grand-mother calling him—clear from another state. Ferlin gave him a hall pass. "For out-standing imagination."

With splendid generosity, she dispersed hall passes to everybody. Soon the room was empty except for Marthur and Ferlin.

"Well then," said Ferlin. "Now that they're all sardined in the bathroom, let's get to our teaching." Her eyes burned like new stars.

Marthur was dying to talk to Ferlin about the miraculous spoon. And the king who was supposedly coming. Why not tell? She and her father would soon be in trouble for blabbing, anyway. But she didn't even have time to open her mouth before Ferlin launched in.

"The first lesson of teaching is written on the board," proclaimed Ferlin.

Marthur looked. She saw nothing but a green expanse.

"I don't see it," she said.

"I said, *the first lesson of teaching is written on the chalkboard*," growled Ferlin.

Instantly, the chalk floated up and scribbled:

No gambling.

"Wrong list!"
The chalk wrote:

You never know
what you're teaching.

Marthur was already confused. "What does that *mean*?"

"Well, imagine you're teaching geography," said Ferlin. "The location of places like Chichicastenango. Ashley throws a spit wad at Sam, so you shout at her. What do your pupils learn?"

"To throw spit wads?" ventured Marthur.

"They learn that it's okay to shout," said Ferlin. "A teacher must be on her toes at all times. Be vigilant. Watch out."

"Gee," said Marthur. "Teaching is *hard*."

"You bet your sweet tooth it is."

Prink! Just then something struck a window. Marthur looked up. *Prink! Prink! Prink! Prink! Prink! Prink! Prink!* Gleams of gravel glanced off the glass. Marthur heard sniggering.

"That Rufus," she grumbled. "Why isn't he in the bathroom with everybody else?

He's spoiling your magnificent lesson. Can't you—"

"Yell at him?" suggested Ferlin. She looked hard at Marthur and raised her eyebrows, which resembled two fuzzy white caterpillars.

Marthur thought about that. "Then he'd learn how to yell—" Under her breath she muttered, "—better."

"Excellent!" said Ferlin. "You've learned Lesson One. Now let's turn Rufus into popcorn and pour butter over him."

Marthur giggled. "That's kind of drastic, isn't it?"

"Perhaps."

"I don't hear him anymore. I think he's gone."

"Good. That saves me some butter. Well, Marthur, that's it for today."

Marthur said, "I love teaching!"

XVIII

Marthur should have been elated about her first teaching lesson. She should have dawdled and danced in the halls and, for fun, tried not to step on cracks. But she had a feeling something bad was going to happen. Her skin felt crawly. She shivered and started walking home fast.

The school halls were empty. And quiet. And spooky. To calm herself down, Marthur began repeating the "hold fast" poem. She was so jittery, she got it pretty mixed up: "Hold fast to dreams. If they croak you're out of luck. When dreams break it snows and snows. Hold fast to birds or you will freeze."

Her father was right. It was a great poem.

"So," a sneery voice said suddenly, "how was your *special* class—with your own *special* teacher?"

Rufus! (In jeans again.) She nearly fell down from fright. But then she thought: *Marthur, you've faced dragons and Klunk and a giant tongue (sort of). You can face brat-boy easily.* Quickly, she gathered herself. She looked at Rufus and imagined—a tub of popcorn, each Rufus-faced kernel oozing with butter. Marthur's fear melted. She wasn't scared. In fact, she was peeved, vexed, incensed, aggravated, exasperated, riled, wroth, and *totally* ticked off.

"You—you—you—*bully*!" she cried. "Why are you always picking on me?"

"I don't like you."

"You don't *know* me."

"I know you're *smart.*" Rufus spit that

out like it was gopher poison. "Now you've got your own special teacher to make you smarter." She could tell it infuriated him.

"Golly!" yelled Marthur. "What is your problem?"

Rufus glared at her. He balled up his fists. He dropped into a threatening crouch. "My dad thinks I'm brainless 'cause I do crummy in school," he mumbled, whiffing a little jab close to her. "He wants me to be—like you," he snarled. (Jab, jab.) "Little miss *brain-o*. I'm gonna kronkle you!" (Jab. Jab, jab, jab.)

So. That was it! You could have knocked Marthur over with a baby's breath.

"Rufus Turk, you're CRAZY! Your father doesn't know me, either!"

Rufus put his arms down, but his fists were still ready. "He sees your stupid mug in the paper. Every time you win a stupid prize.

For spelling. Or math. Or science. I'm sick of hearing 'Be like that kid. She's going someplace.'"

"I STUDY," Marthur said. "Did you ever try that?"

"I'm no good at it. The dancing eggs. They were gonna make me rich. Show my dad how smart I am. But you—you and that witch—"

"She's NOT a witch! She's a teacher. A magnificent one!"

"Magnificent, *magnificent*," Rufus taunted. "You can't even use normal words! *Jeez!*"

"Well, she is."

"Anyways, somehow you weirdos wrecked my dragon deal," Rufus snarled. "But I don't need to study now. I've got another plan. A better one. I'M gonna be king."

"Huh?"

"I'm gonna grab that old spoon," Rufus

said, "so's I can wear a crown, sit on a throne, and be boss of everything. Then my dad'll know I'm *somebody*. And you better not tell—or else." He took one more fake jab at her and stalked off.

Gee-minnooties! *Everybody* was telling her not to tell stuff. Marthur couldn't tell, even if she'd wanted to. She was speechless.

The whole way back to the boiler room, Marthur thought about Rufus. She'd told him he didn't know her. But she didn't know him, either. Poor Rufus. He just wanted to please his father.

When she got home, Marthur stumbled into her pj's. Her belly was grumbling. She'd only had a piece of (stale) cheese for lunch. She looked around for something to eat. On an orange crate, she saw a greasy bag and a note:

My dearest darling dumpling,
Here's a little sumpling.
(Har! Har!)
Love, Daddy

Her father had left her three slices of bacon from the cafeteria.

"I love you, too, Daddy," Marthur said into the air. Then, like a leaky pipe, she burst into tears.

So much was happening, Marthur's mind was a jumble. That night she dreamed that Rufus was wearing a crown and roaring with laughter, watching his minions bury her in trash. And twelve tiny dragons (wearing construction-cone hats like Ferlin's) were lolling on a lunch table, gobbling Jell-O from twelve weird old spoons.

XIX

Marthur woke up feeling as floppy as a sunstroked jellyfish. When she hadn't been dreaming, she'd been wide awake, tossing and thinking stuff like: *Is the spoon for real or just a prank? What if Klunk's king? The kids at school will be really squashed. AGH! So will Daddy! Rufus's father wants him to be smart. What can I do about that? AGH! AGH! AAAAGH!*

At breakfast she stared off and nibbled the last piece of bacon, savoring every tasty morsel. Suddenly she got a brain wave. Actually, she got *two.* Brain-bursting works of staggering genius. "That's IT!" she cried.

"Or do I mean *those* are it?" She spronged up and hustled off to class. She couldn't wait to tell Ferlin. On her way, she passed the bathroom where the famous spoon was lodged.

GOLLY! It was only 7:30 and already a line of would-be royalty was waiting to go into the already sardined bathroom. It was such a huge crush, Marthur could hardly get past. The line looked like it spooled through all the corridors and right around the whole entire school! Everybody was pushing and shoving, antsy to take a crack at yanking out the spoon. It seemed that everybody (even kindergartners) wanted to be king!

The nurse, Ms. Quimper (rhymes with *whimper*), was first in line. (She'd left a sign on her door: OUT TO LUNCH INDEFINITELY. HEAL YOURSELVES.)

The cafeteria staff was there, too. Those staffers probably believed they had special powers, working with utensils and all.

Marthur was relieved. "Whew!" she breathed. "Klunk's not king yet. Neither is Rufus."

Eager to spill her brain waves, Marthur rushed into the science room. "Hi, Ferlin. Hello, Griffin," she said. It was a regal animal, she knew, so she gave it a little bow.

There was nobody else in class.

"You'll be a teacher in a trice. Isn't that nice?" Ferlin chortled. "With everybody at the bathroom acting like ninnies, I've got nothing to do but teach you."

This was Marthur's chance. "You could teach somebody else—" she began.

"Who?"

"Rufus." Marthur blabbled on like a broken hydrant. "His father wants him to be the brainiest. But he can't do that, so he punches me. See? So, can Rufus be in our special class—so he can get smart fast and his father will like *him* and not me? Please? Please! PLEASE with pretty sugar?"

Ferlin looked fondly at Marthur. "You are a very kindhearted girl. I wish that I could say yes. But my job is to teach you—and nobody else—how to teach. There isn't much time left."

Who'd given her that job? Why only Marthur? Why Marthur at all? (Didn't a No. 1 wizard have better things to do?) What did Ferlin mean about time? They had plenty—didn't they? The whole thing was freaky.

Tears shivered in Marthur's eyes. "But Rufus is so unhappy. It's not fair."

"Life's not fair. But that's how it is."

"But why *can't* he be special, too?"

"You'll see," said Ferlin mysteriously.

"Now. Let's proceed with the proceedings. Chalk, Lesson Two!" she ordered.

"Wait," Marthur said. "Just one more thing. I—"

"Think that your father would make a good king?"

Marthur shook herself to make sure this was really happening.

"How did you know?"

"I'm a top-notch wizard, remember?"

"Well, Daddy *would* make a good king. A perfect one. He's so gentle and honest and funny and kind. And he makes up words. And he knows a poem—sort of. And he gets me bacon. All he needs is one chance at the spoon. If I could just get him to the front of the line—"

"Marthur." Ferlin put a hand on her shoulder. "Rufus can't be my pupil. And your father, bless his sweet old heart, can't be king. It is not written."

Marthur was so disappointed, she nearly broke down. But she was a Snapdragon. She stuck out her chin. "What *is* written?"

"Look at the chalkboard," said Ferlin.

Quickly the stubby white stick scrawled:

Don't talk down.

"Watch your penmanship, for heaven snakes!" Ferlin snapped. The board erased itself and the chalk rewrote the sentence—neatly.

Marthur read the lesson. "What does that mean?" she asked as enthusiastically as she could. She was glum about Ferlin turning both Rufus and her father down.

"Talk to kids in a normal way. They're not babies or slobbering spaniels. Just roll along. They'll catch up with you."

"AND I'VE CAUGHT UP TO *YOU*, LITTLE MISSY!"

Crikers! Klunk!

"Pretty hard not to," remarked Ferlin. "She's sitting stone still."

"Don't get smart with me," snapped Dr. Klunk. "Those Snapdragons blatted about the spoon. Just look what they've done!" He jabbed a fat finger at all the people crowding the corridor.

"Marthur and her father didn't peep," Ferlin said.

"Anyway, I'm having them arrested," Klunk spluttered.

"For talking about a spoon? Since when is that a crime?"

All this time the line was getting longer.

"OH, FORGET IT!" Klunk yelled.

"Where are you going?" asked Marthur, worried about the law.

"To butt in line!"

XX

Marthur was sure that, one way or another, the slippery Klunk would get the spoon. Then he would be king. Or Rufus, maybe, if he had his way. Marthur and her father were going to jail. She couldn't stand it. She couldn't concentrate on Lesson Two.

Ferlin looked right at her. "Marthur," she said, "do you want to quit?"

Marthur looked at Ferlin. She felt suddenly calm. She knew she could do this. Slowly she said, "No. No, I don't want to quit. I'm going to be a teacher—no matter what." She added, "Hold fast."

"Good girl!"

Then Ferlin said, "Chalk, lie down! Marthur, you're worn out. Go home. But tomorrow we romp through the rest."

"The rest?"

"The rest of the lessons. You're going to need them all—*soon.*"

"How do you know?"

Ferlin's eyes glowed. "I just DO."

Marthur felt strong. She could learn how to teach; she just knew it.

She walked out of Ferlin's room and into pandemonium. Every class had been canceled because of the spoon. Every kid (and every teacher) at Horace E. Bloggins School had poured into the halls, blathering about kings. Or they were shoving one another around in the ever-growing line, waiting to have a go at the fabulous spoon. (The minions had abandoned Rufus to take their best shot.)

Marthur jostled her way through the milling masses, repeating all she knew about teaching: "You never know what you're teaching." "Don't look down—no! Don't *talk* down."

It was a lot to grasp. Could she ever learn it all? "Hold fast!" she exhorted herself. "Hold fast!"

"Hold up!" hissed a voice.

A holdup! Marthur thought. She nearly collapsed.

It was Rufus. "Thanks," he said gruffly. His face got red.

"Huh?" said Marthur, stupefied.

"I know what you did."

"Huh?"

"Thanks for trying to get me into your stupid special class with your stupid special teacher."

A lightbulb flashed on in Marthur's brain. A BIG one. *Special teacher!* It was the second time he'd said that. That was it! Marthur blurted, "You could have a teacher of your own."

"Who?"

"Me. I could help you with school."

"I don't need help," Rufus snarled.

"So be a dope."

"Well, maybe I could use a *teensy* bit," Rufus admitted slowly.

"Okay," said Marthur. "I'll tutor you—if you leave me and my father alone."

"Deal—if you keep your trap shut about it."

Marthur stuck her hand out. "Shake," she said.

"No way." Rufus looked at her like she had cooties.

"When do we start?" he asked.

"Tomorrow night," said Marthur. "At my place. Bring your math book."

For the time being Marthur could relax—as long as she helped Rufus. But as a teacher with only two lessons under her belt, she was pretty green. She was glad that the next day she'd learn the rest about teaching.

XXI

The next day Marthur raced to Ferlin's room.

"What are the rest?" she asked, dashing in.

Ferlin's eyebrows shot up. "Could you be a bit more vague?"

Marthur blushed. "The rest of the lessons," she said timidly. "I could use them. I'm—er—uh—teaching somebody."

"Good grief, you're an eager beaver!" Ferlin said. She sounded peeved, but her eyes twinkled. In a swirl, she turned to face the chalkboard. "Let's have them all!" she commanded.

The chalk levitated, then feverishly wrote (in cursive):

*Ferlin's Perfect Rules
of Teaching*

*1. You never know
what you're teaching.*

"You already know that one," Ferlin said.

2. Don't talk down.

"Ditto."

*3. Homework should not be
synonymous with torture.*

"Easy," said Marthur.

4. Make lessons MAGNIFICENT.

"You mean wild?"

"I mean unforgettable."

"Like the dancing eggs?"

"Precisely." Ferlin smiled. "You're doing nicely."

5. Keep alive.

"Don't die in class?" Marthur asked.

"Try not to do that, heaven knows. But embrace learning. Soak it up. So will your pupils."

6. Humiliation is highly unacceptable.

"Teachers hold places of power," said Ferlin. "To make pupils feel small is despicable."

"Like bullying?"

"Bravo, my Marthur!"

7. Every pupil is of value.

"Self-explanatory."

8. Every pupil is of <u>equal</u> value.

"Like Rufus?"
"Everybody."

9. Learn from your pupils.

"Yeah," Marthur agreed. "Kids know a ton of stuff."

10. Mercy is highly acceptable.

"When you get a chance to be kind, grab it," said Ferlin.

Marthur said, "I like that one."

11. One to grow on: Laugh a lot.

"I just tossed that in." Ferlin laughed her head off.

Marthur suddenly panicked. "What if I mess up?" She worried about Rufus. Maybe she'd ruin him.

"You have tomorrow—and tomorrow and tomorrow—to do better."

Throughout the lesson it had been weirdly quiet. No sign of Rufus. No sniggers. No snorts. No stones hitting the windows. Marthur wondered if Ferlin had cast a spell around her room—to keep him away for once.

It was very strange. Marthur's mind was so riveted on the lessons, she never once thought about the coming of the king or the spoon.

Ferlin clapped like a firecracker. A copy of "Ferlin's Perfect Rules of Teaching" flew into Marthur's hands.

"Well, there you have it, dear Marthur,"

said Ferlin. "All you need to know about teaching."

"That's it?"

"Yep. Study them well and you'll be ready—for anything."

Funny. It sounded like Ferlin meant more than teaching.

"By the way," Ferlin said as Marthur was leaving, "I've decided to relent about Rufus."

"Golly day! Thanks!"

"If you can help him, I can, too. He won't be my pupil. Not like you. But I'll give him some dragon work to do."

"Like what?"

"Don't be so nosy." Then Ferlin added mysteriously, "You'll see."

XXII

Porta Potties had sprung up at school like bright blue mushrooms.

"What're those doing here?" Marthur asked Rufus. She'd been tutoring him in the boiler room. Day after day, whenever she could. On fractions and stuff like that. Using Ferlin's Rules to keep on track. Nobody went to class anymore (and nobody cared) but Rufus and her. Who would've believed it?

Rufus was doing okay. He was actually trying. (So hard sometimes, he even got headaches.) He'd pretty much dumped his thuggy friends. He was still gruff, but with less huff and puff. Of course, it didn't hurt that Ferlin was giving him dragon work (whatever that was). Because of it, he always smelled like smoke. And sometimes his eyebrows—or his clothes—were singed. Funny thing, he wasn't after the spoon anymore.

Now they were outside taking a break. Rufus told Marthur, "Klunk hired a wrestler, Slam-Bam Sammy" (rhymes with *whammy*).

"How come?"

"To loosen the spoon for him. Sammy sweated and grunted and strained like crazy. But the spoon didn't budge. Slam-Bam Sammy got so mad, he stamped his feet and blubbered like a baby."

Marthur grinned at that.

"After Slam-Bam's failure, Klunk gave a big fat order," Rufus said. "KEEP YOUR STINKING HANDS OFF THE SPOON! Nobody's allowed in the boys' bathroom but him."

"So it's Porta Potties or bushes?"

"You got it," said Rufus. "The kids and teachers planned to swarm the bathroom today. Take over. But Klunk outsmarted them."

"How?"

"He's called in Grease-ball Burgers. Free burgers all around. He can work away at the spoon while everybody eats."

"Aim for the stomach," joked Marthur.

A roar filled the Horace E. Bloggins parking lot. Three Grease-ball Burgers trucks rolled up. Cheers erupted from students and teachers as guys in white caps began doling out free eats.

"Gotta go," said Rufus.

"What about fractions?"

"Burgers first." He cracked a crooked smile and ran.

Marthur didn't feel like a burger. Or anything. Not even bacon.

All she could think of was Dr. Klunk somehow jimmying the spoon from the bathroom wall. Somehow becoming king. She scuffed along the halls lost in those dark thoughts.

Then, by chance (or was it?), Marthur found herself outside the boys' bathroom. The door was blocked by barbed wire and lots of prickery cactus. Everything was still.

Then a bloodcurdling yell came from inside. Dr. Klunk!

"HELP! IT'S GOING TO EAT ME ALIVE!"

What was going to eat him? The spoon? How could a spoon eat anything? Marthur didn't ponder that long. Dodging the prickers, she just rocketed in.

XXIII

Marthur skidded in and found Dr. Klunk cowering in a corner. He was shrieking the tiles off the walls. "It's gonna eat me alive! It's gonna eat me alive!"

Ferlin's grimly griffin loomed beside Klunk, booming a ditty as if it were a hymn:

> *"Forsooth I shall eat thee, thou wretched*
> *   foul man.*
> *I'll devour thee so sweetly—and SLOW*
> *   as I can.*
> *First I'll rip off thine head, then rend*
> *   thine black heart.*
> *O' hey, nonny nonny, the feast will be*
> *   bonny.*

*O' hey, nonny nonny, is't thou ready to
start?"*

Its tawny eyes glowed. Its razor beak
gleamed. Its sickle claws glinted. The fig-
loving beast was about to seize him (and
squeeze him) like a great big fig and devour
him, wraparounds and all! Poor Dr. Klunk!
Marthur didn't like him, but she didn't
want him *eaten*!

"STOP!" she yelped. She looked around
wildly for something to fend off the griffin—but not injure him. And so it was, in a
mad lunge, that Marthur grabbed for the
spoon.

"Spoon," she cried in a frazzle, "I *really*
need you! Not for me! But for my principal!"

The room grew oddly quiet. So did
Klunk. Marthur could almost feel the silence. Like light. Time hung suspended.

Marthur felt strange. And wistful, holding this fistful of mysterious spoon. Then an eerie humming—a silvery tintinnabulation—began spooling through the boys' bathroom, so beautiful it wrenched her heart. It sounded like music from afar—like the lovely thrumming of a star.

"Please, spoon, come out," Marthur pleaded, her eyes brimming. "Dr. Klunk is about to be eaten." She thought of her father's worthy poem, and she held fast. Marthur closed her eyes. She tugged on the handle with all she could muster. The spoon slipped out, as though it had been stuck in butter.

The spell was broken. The griffin sniffed Klunk's coat. Then, as delicately as a lady tasting tea cakes at a party, it plucked a fig from Klunk's lumpy pocket, ate the sweet fruit, and ambled out.

Marthur stared at the beautiful spoon glittering and glowing in her hand. She was absolutely and utterly mystified. Slam-Bam Sammy (and everybody else) must have loosened it up.

Klunk suddenly came to himself. "I HATE figs!" he snarled. "My pockets are stuffed with the rotten things! Who planted that beast bait on me? I bet it was that infernal Ferlin woman!"

Then Dr. Klunk looked down. He saw the wondrous spoon in Marthur's hand. His eyes bulged like an evil toad's. He licked his chops and leered from ear to ugly ear.

"Well, well, well," he sneered. "What have we here?"

XXIV

Dr. Klunk snatched the spoon from Marthur. He grinned grotesquely.

"Thanks, little missy." And he hotfooted it for the office.

Klunk snapped on the school loudspeaker and blurted: "Attention! Stop stuffing your faces, everybody! Get to the auditorium!"

His voice screaked like a short circuit. Everybody moved quick. (Even the burger guys.) Maybe an earthquake was coming. Or a tidal wave. Or an invasion of frogs. In no time, all of Horace E. Bloggins School was packed into the auditorium.

"I yanked the spoon from the bathroom wall! See?" Klunk blustered, waving it like a shillelagh. "I now proclaim myself—"

"The fattest liar on the face of the earth!" blared Rufus. "I saw the whole thing. Marthur pulled out that old spoon!"

The throng gasped so deeply, it nearly sucked all the air from the room. Marthur was flabbergasted (and touched) that Rufus had spoken up for her.

"He's spouting bunk!" shouted Klunk.

Rufus had a reputation for prevarication. So now—heavens to mercy!—nobody believed him! It got very quiet in the auditorium. Everybody looked worried out of his mind. Holy hasenpfeffers! Klunk was going to be king. Nothing could stop him!

Suddenly the air rang like a gong. "Feign not, blackguard! I, too, bear witness," intoned a voice that only a Spoon of Power could possess. It was passionately angry. It was a right regal spoon and would not brook the shenanigans of the blasted buffoon.

With a wrench, it wrested itself from Klunk's grasp. For a moment it shivered in midair right in his face. Then—it thwacked him on the head, like cracking a great big hard-boiled egg.

"Ow!"

Klunk ran.

The archaical (but nimble) spoon gave chase.

"Rotter! Rogue! Rascal! Scoundrel! Scalawag! Wretch! Blackguard! Churl! Miscreant! Villain! Vile varlet! Blot! Blight! Blister! Plague! Calumnious knave!" it raged.

Whack! It smacked him again.

"Ow!"

Whack! Whack! Whack!

"Ow! Ow! Ow!"

Everybody cheered.

"Enough!" cried Marthur. "Stop!"

At once the venerable spoon obeyed.

"Your wish is my command, O faire liege lady-king."

It slipped itself into her hand.

"I am called X-Cauliflower, Your Highness," the spoon apprised her. (*X-C*, Marthur realized. *Like on the egg carton!*)

"I am called Marthur," whispered Marthur shyly.

She glanced up. She saw her dear father beaming at her—and crying. She saw all the kids she'd ever helped cheering and cheering. She saw Ferlin arrayed in full regalia, smiling and proudly twirling her mustache. (That is, she would have been if she'd had one. She was twirling a frizzy hank of hair.)

Ferlin looked at Marthur with love. "Hail!" she said.

"Please, don't do that." Marthur blushed.

"Looky there!" somebody shouted. Twelve eggs, now solid gold, came razzmatazzing in. Rufus was with them. He waved his hands just so, and the eggs split open to reveal twelve golden dragons, fizzing and spritzing like sparklers.

"Behold the Dragons of the Realm," said Ferlin, as the creatures swelled, bigger and bigger. "They will protect you from anything, my king—and provide fine fireworks for your coronation."

"They're good at that." Marthur laughed. "But I can't be king," she whispered, embarrassed by the fuss. "All I did was pull out a spoon."

"Ah! But you acted out of mercy and kindness," said Ferlin. "Just what a good monarch needs. You could have let the griffin gobble Klunk."

"I can't be king," Marthur insisted. "I'm only ten. I don't know anything."

Ferlin said gently, "The rules for kinging are pretty much like the rules for teaching."

Marthur was amazed. She finally said, "Except for homework?"

"That's up to you, King Marthur."

And so (Hold fast!) Marthur's dream came true. Though she was not a teacher, she was a king—which was more or less the same.

XXV

What a magnificent time for the Snapdragon family! For everybody!

One week later, amid a great hubbub of excitement (with X-Cauliflower beside her), King Marthur took charge of Horace E. Bloggins School.

Immediately, King Marthur made some changes:

She gave illuminated textbooks to every single kid at Bloggins. She asked the woodshop class to make a round table, so there would be no special seats at meetings. She made Dr. Klunk the janitor. Her adored father became principal. (Not many schools

had a principal *and* a king, but the Snapdragons were a team.) Of course, Ferlin remained Marthur's dear adviser.

What about Rufus Turk? He was named
the Bloggins Dragon Keeper, in charge of all
school special effects. For "gallantly bearing
witness under no duress whatsoever," Ferlin
presented Rufus with his own personal
dragon. (That really wowed his father!)

Last, so that no kid would ever go hungry, King Marthur proclaimed:

The cafeteria will forever serve—
FREE BACON!